GOING TO SCHOOL

By Rose Blake

Frances Lincoln
Children's Books

Today I am going to school.

My friends travel to school in lots of different ways,

but I like to ride my scooter best.

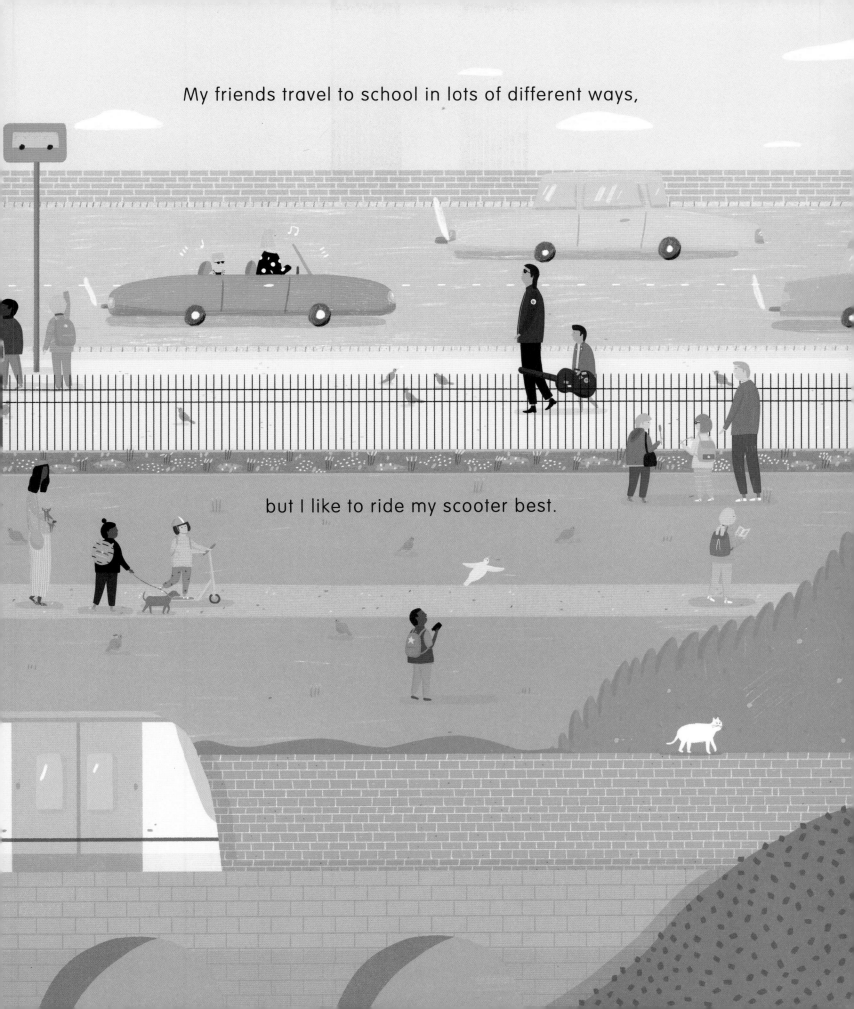

I arrive at the school gate just as the bell rings.

"Goodbye!" I say, and run inside.

This is our teacher, Miss Balmer.

"Hello!"

I hang up my coat and bag, and go inside the classroom.

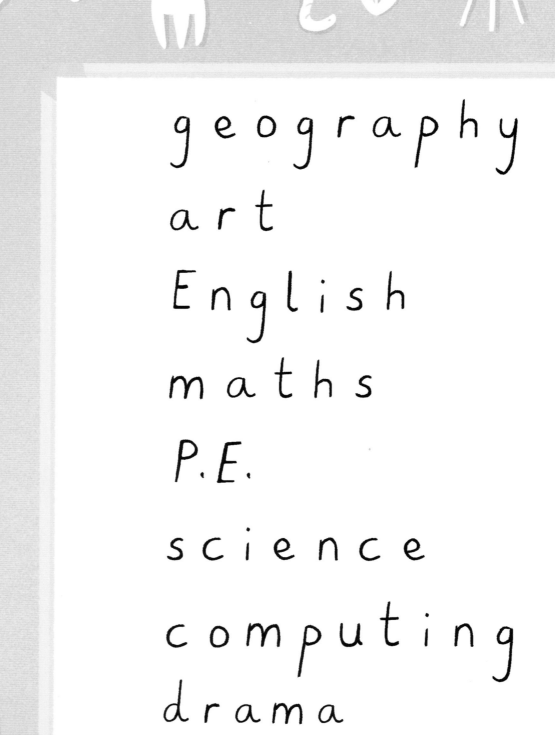

geography

art

English

maths

P.E.

science

computing

drama

Miss Balmer has written what we'll be
doing today on the whiteboard.

Miss Balmer

✓ Katrina	✓ Paloma
✓ Frankie	✓ Erik
✓ Milo	✓ Grace
✓ Jenny	✓ Sid
✓ Liam	✓ Ammu
✓ Josh	✓ Greta
✓ Rose	Zoe
✓ Sonny	Tommy
✓ Alex	Frank

At nine o'clock
we're ready to start.

Our first lesson is about
the world around us.

We learn about giant mountains and huge lakes.

Miss Balmer rolls out a map of the world, and we show each
other where some of our friends and family come from.

Art is my favourite lesson. We can make elephants out of plastic bottles,
a flock of colourful tropical birds, or a giant cardboard robot.

Today, some of us are making paper masks. Mine is a big, round moon!

The bell rings and it's break time.

In the playground, we can swing on the climbing frame, play football, or show off our best yoyo tricks.

I take turns skipping with
Tommy and Katrina.

After break, it's time for reading and writing. Today, Miss Balmer is reading us a story in the Book Nook.

When I close my eyes and listen, I feel like I'm flying through a starry sky, over a sleeping city.

Your imagination can take you to lots of exciting places when you're reading! What's your favourite story?

Then it's time for maths. We use the blocks to help us count, solve puzzles and play fun number games.

Miss Balmer shows us how to tell the time on the clocks, and some of us play a shopping game to practise using numbers in real life.

TODAY'S SHOPPING LIST:

3 BANANAS - 10P
RED PEPPER - 70P
CHEESE - £2
2 CARROTS -
WATERMEL
6 EGGS - £1

In P.E. we put on our gym kit and run, climb, jump and stretch. Sometimes, we play team games, like football and basketball.

Greta can spin three hula hoops at a time!

Peep peep!
Miss Balmer blows
her whistle and it's
time for...

Lunch! We queue up and choose what we want to eat. I'm hungry!

I'm having chicken curry with rice, a crunchy apple... and a bar of chocolate for desert!

There are lots of different options to choose from. Tommy has spaghetti and a banana, and Katrina has fish, salad and an iced bun.

What do you like to eat for lunch?

After lunch we meet outside the science room and get ready for our next lesson.

There's lots to do! I check on the cress we have been growing...

CHICKS

and Frank waters the sunflowers. We are having a competition to see who can grow the tallest sunflower from a tiny seed. All you need is light and water!

Next, we spend time on the computers. I make some artwork,

but you can also play games, learn about nature, or make your own music!

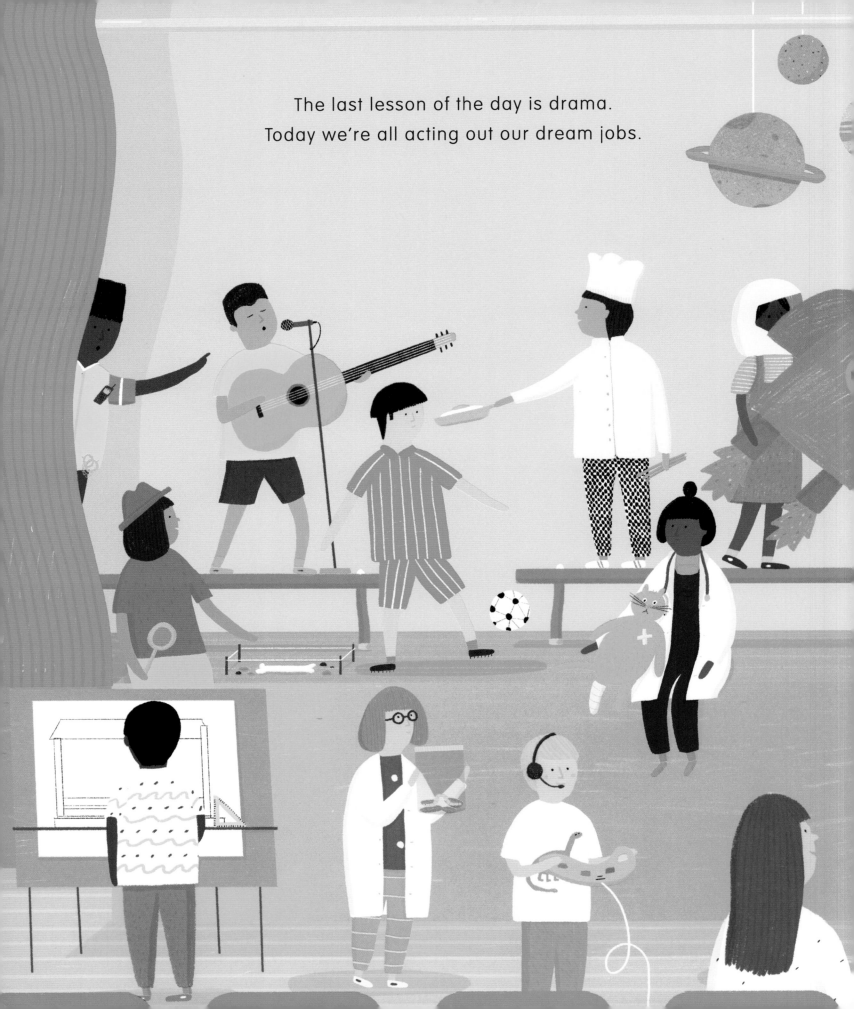

The last lesson of the day is drama.
Today we're all acting out our dream jobs.

When I grow up, I want to be an artist like my Mum.

Can you tell what my friends would like to be? See if you can find any clues in the earlier lessons, too.

At the end of the afternoon,
the bell rings and it's time to go home.

Mum is waiting to pick me up at the gate.
She asks me what I did today.
"Not much," I say.

But I can't wait for tomorrow.

Going to school is great!

For P.B. and C.B. - R.B.

Quarto is the authority on a wide range of topics.

Quarto educates, entertains and enriches the lives of
our readers—enthusiasts and lovers of hands-on living.

www.quartoknows.com

First published in Great Britain in 2017 by Frances Lincoln Children's Books,
74-77 White Lion Street, London N1 9PF, UK
QuartoKnows.com • Visit our blogs at QuartoKnows.com

Text and illustrations copyright © Rose Blake 2017

A catalogue record for this book is available from the British Library.

ISBN 978-1-84780-898-1

Illustrated digitally.
Designed by Nicola Price. Edited by Jenny Broom
Published by Rachel Williams • Production by Dawn Cameron

Printed in China

1 3 5 7 9 8 6 4 2

MIX
Paper from
responsible sources
FSC® C008047

Swimmer

Chef

Film-maker

Vet

Fashion
Designer

Biologist

Artist

Pilot

Game
Designer